First published in the United States and Canada in 2014 by Lemniscaat USA LLC • New York
Distributed in the United States by Lemniscaat USA LLC • New York

te Loo, Sanne.
The Mermaid's Shoes / Sanne te Loo
1. Mermaids–Juvenile fiction. 2. Dreams–Juvenile fiction. 3. Social media–Juvenile literature.
PZ7 [E]

ISBN 978-1-935954-35-4 (Hardcover)
Printed in the United States by Worzalla, Stevens Point, Wisconsin

www.lemniscaatusa.com

The Mermaid's Shoes

Sanne te Loo

Lemniscaat

Mia said goodbye to the sea on the last day of vacation.

She was looking for shells to take home. What was that
lying in the sand? Had someone forgotten something?
Mia was curious. She took a closer look. "Mermaid's
shoes!" she thought. They fit perfectly.

Mia was tired after the long journey home.
The rumble of the traffic reminded
her of the murmur of the sea.
It seemed so long ago when she
played in the waves.

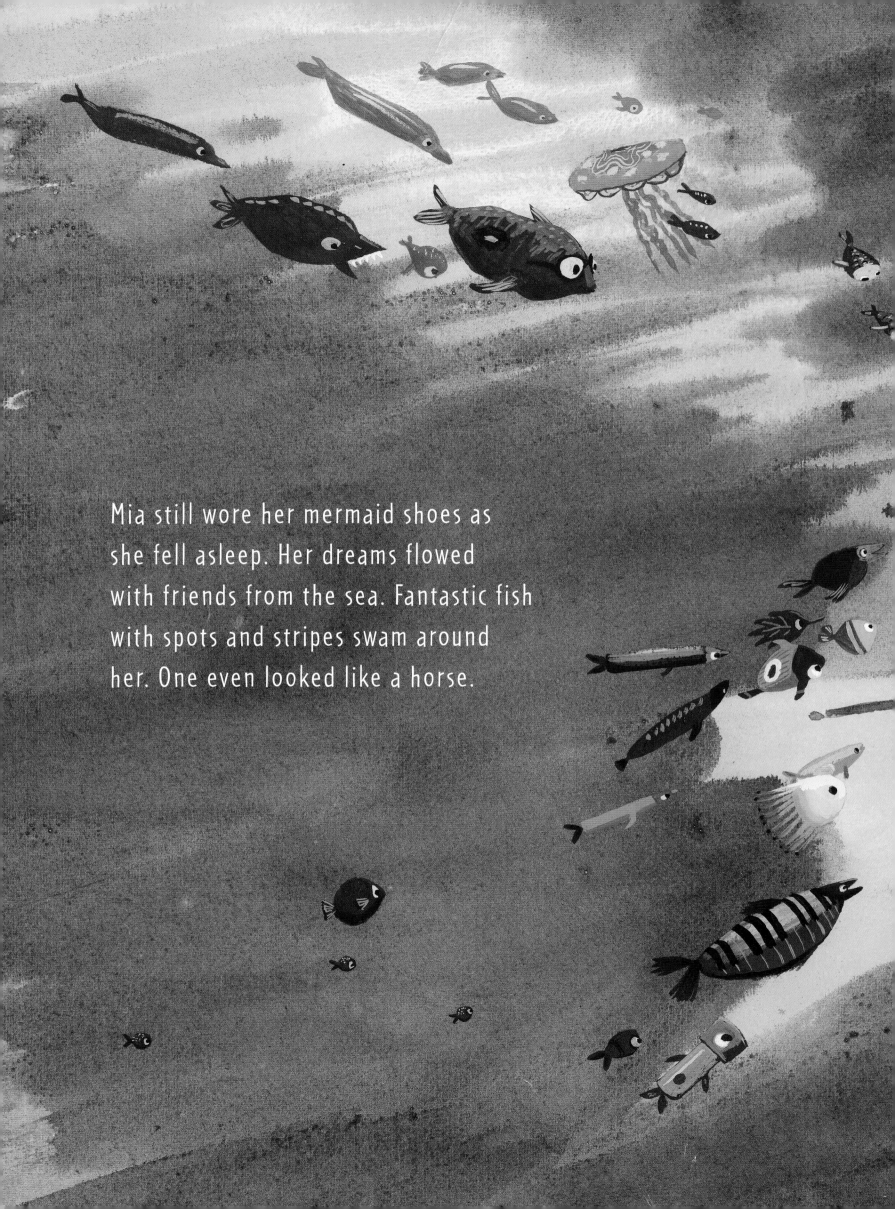

Mia still wore her mermaid shoes as she fell asleep. Her dreams flowed with friends from the sea. Fantastic fish with spots and stripes swam around her. One even looked like a horse.

Mia kept her new shoes on even
in the playground. Her friends
were astonished. "What have you
got on your feet?" they asked.
"I'm a mermaid," said Mia.
"These are my fins."

"They can't be," said Tommy.
"You haven't got a tail."

One thing was missing.

Mia made a mermaid's tail out of one of her mother's old skirts.

To the sea!
It was much too far away so Mia rode
her bike to the zoo. She knew a sea was there.
She had been before.

It was just like walking on the bottom of the sea.

Mia had forgotten about the scary fish with the teeth. Would it eat mermaids?

Mia rode her bike to the river. She leaned over the railing and peered into the water below. There were no big fish with teeth there, but it seemed very deep.

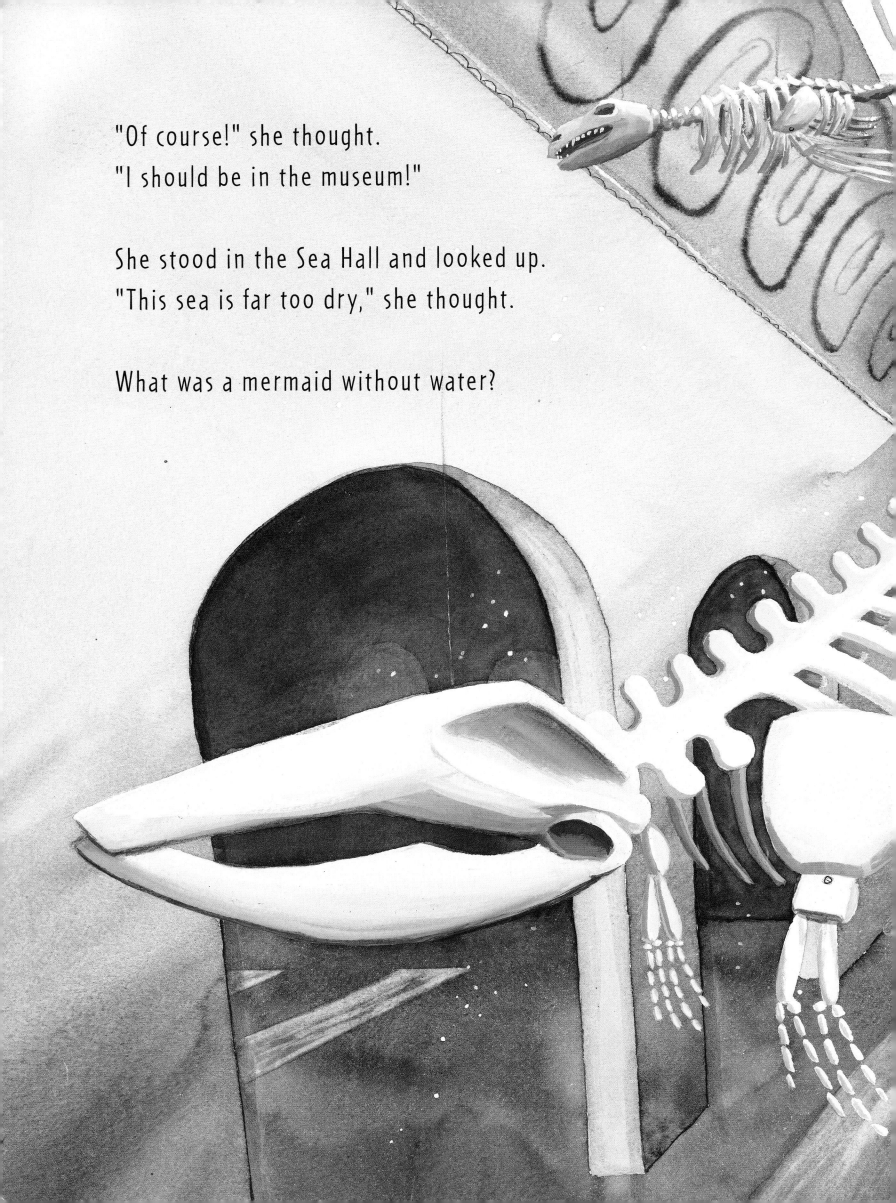

"Of course!" she thought.
"I should be in the museum!"

She stood in the Sea Hall and looked up.
"This sea is far too dry," she thought.

What was a mermaid without water?

Mia gave up. She couldn't find the sea.
She rode home.

Then she heard a gentle murmur. Riding around
the corner, she felt drops of water splash gently
on her face. She saw the most wonderful creatures.
There was even a fish that looked like a horse.
She left her bike and climbed over the edge.

And that's how it began.

http://www.lemniscaat-usa.com